A Note to Parents

For many children, learning math is difficult and "I hate math!" is their first response — to which many parents silently add "Me, too!" Children often see adults comfortably reading and writing, but they rarely have such models for mathematics. And math fear can be catching!

The easy-to-read stories in this *Hello Math* series were written to give children a positive introduction to mathematics and parents a pleasurable re-acquaintance with a subject that is important to everyone's life. *Hello Math* stories make mathematical ideas accessible, interesting, and fun for children. The activities and suggestions at the end of each book provide parents with a hands-on approach to help children develop mathematical interest and confidence.

Enjoy the mathematics!

- Give your child a chance to retell the story. The more familiar children are with the story, the more they will understand its mathematical concepts.
- Use the colorful illustrations to help children "hear and see" the math at work in the story.
- Treat the math activities as games to be played for fun. Follow your child's lead. Spend time on those activities that engage your child's interest and curiosity.
- Activities, especially ones using physical materials, help make abstract mathematical ideas concrete.

Learning is a messy process and learning about math calls for children to become immersed in lively experiences that help them make sense of mathematical concepts and symbols.

Although learning about numbers is basic to math, other ideas, such as identifying shapes and patterns, measuring, collecting and interpreting data, reasoning logically, and thinking about chance are also important. By reading these stories and having fun with the activities, you will help your child enthusiastically say "*Hello, Math*," instead of "I hate math."

—Marilyn Burns
National Mathematics Educator
Author of *The I Hate Mathematics! Book*

To my wife, Rhona
—J.Z.

ISBN 0-590-60246-2
Copyright © 1996 by Scholastic Inc.
The activities on pages 27-32 copyright © 1996 by Marilyn Burns.
All rights reserved. Published by Scholastic Inc.
CARTWHEEL BOOKS and the CARTWHEEL BOOKS logo
are registered trademarks of Scholastic Inc.
HELLO MATH READER and the HELLO MATH READER logo
are trademarks of Scholastic Inc.

Library of Congress Cataloging-in-Publication Data
Nagel, Karen Berman.
    The lunch line / by Karen Nagel; illustrated by Jerry Zimmerman; math activities by Marilyn Burns.
        p.   cm. — (Hello math reader. Level 3)
    Summary: In the school cafeteria at lunchtime, Kim eyes all the tasty food and tries to figure out what she can buy with her dollar.
    ISBN 0-590-60246-2
    [1. Money — Fiction. 2. School lunchrooms, cafeterias, etc. — Fiction. 3. Food — Fiction.] I. Zimmerman, Jerry, ill. II. Title. III. Series.
PZ7.N1345Lu   1996
[E] — dc20   96-14354
                                                                  CIP
                                                                  AC

12 11 10 9 8 7 6 5 4 3   7 8 9/9 0 1/0
              Printed in the U.S.A.   09
          First Scholastic printing, September 1996

The Lunch Line

by Karen Berman Nagel
Illustrated by Jerry Zimmerman
Math Activities by Marilyn Burns

Hello Math Reader — Level 3

SCHOLASTIC INC.
New York Toronto London Auckland Sydney

The hands on the clock
stood straight up.
The lunch bell rang.
Kim's stomach
growled.

Feed me!

She thought about her
peanut butter sandwich,
and her cookies,
and her banana.

Her stomach
growled again.

She reached for her lunch bag.

It wasn't there.

Or here.

She must have left it
on the bus.

Now she would have to buy
her lunch — for the very first time.

Kim checked her left pocket
and found two quarters.
She checked her right pocket
and found five dimes.

Was that enough for lunch?

"Let's go!" the teacher said.

Kim got in line behind
her friend Sarah.
"Is one dollar enough money
for lunch?" she whispered.

"Can't talk now," Sarah said.
"I have to keep my eye on
that peanut butter sandwich."

While Kim looked at the menu,
Jeff cut in front of her.

"I'll have the meat surprise,
the potato surprise,
the fruit surprise,
and the ice cream surprise,"
Jeff said.

Jeff paid $4.
He didn't get any change.

"Hmm, maybe I should buy
the meat surprise," Kim said.

She looked at Jeff's plate.

Maybe pizza would be better.

The lunch worker was waiting
for Kim to decide.

I could get two slices of pizza,
Kim thought.

But what if I get thirsty?

"Let's buy popcorn," Matt said.
"No, I want corn chips," Pat said.

"I have 20 cents," said Matt.
"So? I have a quarter," said Pat.

Matt looked in his sneaker.
He found a nickel.

"Now I have 25 cents, too," he said.

"Forget it," said Pat.
"Let's buy snacks after school."

Matt and Pat didn't buy anything.

Kim looked at the
two quarters
and five dimes in her hands.
They were damp.
She was really hungry.

Kim's stomach flip-flopped.

"I'll have apple juice and
an oatmeal cookie," she whispered.
Her hands shook.
She heard the
quarters banging
against the dimes.

"And I'll have the . . .
the . . . "

There they were!
"The . . . "

"Fish sticks,
please," said Alex.

"Those are *my* fish sticks!"
Kim cried.

"I asked for them first," said Alex.

"But I bought an apple juice
and an oatmeal cookie.
I only have 50 cents left," said Kim.

"*You* got the last oatmeal cookie?"
cried Alex.

Alex looked at Kim.
Kim looked at Alex.
They both looked at their trays.
They both looked at the menu.

"Do you like grilled cheese?"
asked Alex.
"Yes," answered Kim.

"I'll get that and give you half,"
he said. "You get the fish sticks
and give me two."

"And we'll split the cookie!"
they said at the same time.

Learning to make purchases and figuring change is a necessary life skill for children. The story and activities in this book provide a way to give your child a firmer grasp on calculating with money. They also give a context for talking with your child about the responsibility of making purchases.

To help your child be successful with the activities in this book, have real money available. You'll notice that the game *Race for $1* (page 31) calls for a $1 bill and an assortment of coins (25 to 30 pennies, 5 to 10 nickels, 5 to 10 dimes, 2 or 3 quarters). This collection of money comes in handy with other activities as well.

If you find that your child enjoys the story, but the activities are too difficult to tackle, take some time to talk about the value of coins and how to figure with money. Then, if your child is interested, try the activities again.

Be sure to involve your child as you make purchases at the supermarket and in other stores. The more experiences your child has, the better he or she will be prepared to cope with real-life situations on his or her own. Be open to your child's interests, and have fun with math!

— Marilyn Burns

You'll find tips and suggestions for guiding the activities whenever you see a box like this!

Retelling the Story

When Kim checked her left pocket, she found two quarters. Can you tell how much money that is?

When she checked her right pocket, she found five dimes. Can you tell how much money that is?

How much money did Kim have altogether?

It's common for young children not to know the value of coins, so don't worry if your child doesn't know how much money Kim had. Use this activity as an opportunity to help your child learn about how much coins are worth and to show how to figure out totals. Also, you'll find the Hello Math Reader *A Quarter from the Tooth Fairy* useful for helping your child learn about coins and their values.

Matt had 20 cents. What coins can make 20 cents?

When Matt found a nickel in his sneaker, he then had 25 cents. His twin, Pat, had a quarter. Can you explain why they both then had the same amount of money?

When Kim bought an apple juice, an oatmeal cookie, and fish sticks, how much did she spend?

Alex bought apple juice and a grilled cheese sandwich. How much did he spend?

How did Alex and Kim share their lunches?

What Can You Buy for $1?

Can you think of different ways Kim could have spent her $1 on lunch? Figure out different ideas for lunches that cost no more than $1. You may want to keep track on a piece of paper.

If you were in the lunch line, what would you like to buy for lunch? How much would you spend?

Fish Stick Problems

Kim spent 50 cents for four fish sticks.
How much would eight fish sticks cost?
How much would two fish sticks cost?

Here are some harder fish stick problems.
What do you think the cafeteria would
charge for just one fish stick?
How many fish sticks could Kim buy with
75 cents?

Skip these problems if your child isn't interested
or if they seem too difficult. Figuring how much
one fish stick costs requires dividing 25 cents
in half, resulting in 12 1/2 cents, an impossible
amount of money. But this is like the real-life
situation when lemons are priced 3 for $1 and
you want to buy only two.

Race for $1

This is a game for two or more people. The object is to be the first person to get enough coins to trade in for the $1 bill. It's fine to have extra coins, but you must have at least $1.

To play, you need two dice, a $1 bill, and lots of coins (25 to 30 pennies, 5 to 10 nickels, 5 to 10 dimes, 2 or 3 quarters). Set the dollar bill aside. Put all the coins in a pile. Everyone should take turns.

1. On your turn, roll the dice. The sum tells you how much to take from the coin pile.

2. You can also use your turn to exchange some of your coins. (10 pennies for 1 dime, 2 dimes and 1 nickel for a quarter, etc.)

3. Give the dice to the next player and follow the same rules.

4. Play until one player has enough to exchange for the $1 bill.

Remember:

You may exchange only when it's your turn.

Watch to make sure you agree with what the other players do.